A Christmas Special from Postman Pat

Postman Pat™
and the Christmas Baby

John Cunliffe
Illustrated by Stuart Trotter

from the original television designs by **Ivor Wood**

Hodder
Children's
Books

a division of Hodder Headline plc

More Postman Pat adventures:

Postman Pat and the Mystery Tour
Postman Pat and the Beast of Greendale
Postman Pat and the robot
Postman Pat takes flight
Postman Pat and the big surprise
Postman Pat paints the ceiling
Postman Pat has too many parcels
Postman Pat and the suit of armour
Postman Pat and the hole in the road
Postman Pat has the best village
Postman Pat misses the show
Postman Pat follows a trail
Postman Pat in a muddle

First published 1998
by Hodder Children's Books,
a division of Hodder Headline plc
338 Euston Road, London NW1 3BH

Story copyright © 1998 Ivor Wood and John Cunliffe
Text copyright © 1998 John Cunliffe
Illustrations copyright © 1998 Hodder Children's Books
and Woodland Animations Ltd.

ISBN 0 340 69811 X
10 9 8 7 6 5 4 3 2 1

A catalogue record for this book is available
from the British Library.
The right of John Cunliffe to be identified as the
Author of this Work has been asserted by him.

Printed in Italy

There was a lot of snow in Greendale.

"It looks like being a white Christmas!" said Pat, when he met Doctor Gilbertson one frosty morning.

"Yes," said Doctor Gilbertson, "and I'm worried about these roads getting blocked."

"Never mind," said Pat, "the post always gets through."

"Never mind *your* deliveries, what about mine!"said the doctor.

"There's something better than a parcel on the way, and it looks like arriving just in time for Christmas."

"Whatever can it be?" said Pat.

"Peter and Jenny's baby, of course!"

"So soon?" said Pat. "Goodness me, a Christmas baby!"

"Yes, you know how the road blocks up, on the hill, and there's that awkward corner by the barn . . ."

"Don't you worry," said Pat, "Peter'll be able to keep it clear with his tractor."
"I hope he can," said the doctor. "We don't want the ambulance getting stuck when the time comes . . . babies can't wait for a bit of snow, you know!"

"Neither can I," said Pat. "I'd better be on my way! Cheerio!"
"Bye, Pat!"

Pat was on his way.

The road up to Peter Fogg's cottage was a bit tricky, but Jenny was cosy enough, with a good warm fire, and plenty of hot drinks. Peter was out on the tractor when Pat arrived, clearing the road with the snow-plough fitted.
"Never fear, I'll keep it clear!" said Peter.

The snow seemed to get deeper as the day went on.
Pat got his van through all right, with a bit of slipping
and slithering, and a spot of digging out here and there.

Christmas was getting near, and so was the time for the baby.
Doctor Gilbertson popped in to see Jenny, and she had a good look
at the road as well.

"Baby's doing fine," said the doctor, "but what about that snow?
I think we'll book the ambulance for tomorrow, just to be on the safe
side. Then, if that road does get blocked, you'll be safe in Pencaster
Hospital when the youngster arrives."

But Doctor Gilbertson was too late!

It snowed all night.
It snowed as never before.
When morning came, the road
was well and truly blocked.
The snow-plough got as far
as the village, then it got stuck.

Peter couldn't even get to the
barn to get his tractor out!

What were they going to do?
The ambulance would be able
to get as far as the village,
and no further.

Alf managed to get his tractor out,
and he went to see if he could get through
to Peter's cottage. It was no good at all.
The snow was just too deep.

Alf, and Ted, and Pat, and everyone who could carry a spade, began digging to try and clear the road. They were half way, then it began to snow again. As fast as they dug, the snow filled up again behind them.

"If we go on like this," said Alf, "we'll all be trapped."
"We'd best get back to the village while we can," said Ted.

They all gathered in the village hall to decide what to do. The Reverend Timms made hot mugs of coffee for everyone, and they sat round the stove, looking out at the falling snow.

Doctor Gilbertson came in to see if there was a coffee to spare.

"This is really serious," she said. "We'll have to get Jenny to Pencaster."

Then Pat had an idea.

"Don't you remember?" he said. "That time we went up to George's place when he was snowed in?"

"Aye," said Alf, "we took a load of groceries up on that old sledge of mine."

"And came back at top speed," said Pat, laughing.

"And then another time," said Ted, "you borrowed my skis to deliver the post."

"Sledges and skis?" said Doctor Gilbertson. "You can't take a pregnant mother on a sledge, or on skis. Far too risky."

"But what if we could make a special sledge?" said Pat. "A big one, with a seat, and a safety-belt and brakes, so it wouldn't bump into anything? It would be smooth enough on this snow – smoother than the ambulance."

"Well . . ." said Doctor Gilbertson.

"How long would it take to make one?" said Pat.

"If everybody helped," said Ted, "we could do it in a day or two. I've got plenty of wood and stuff, and Pat could whizz to Pencaster on the skis if we need anything."

"You can use our pony to pull it," said Katy and Tom.

"It *might* be in time," said Doctor Gilbertson. "And the ambulance could pick Jenny up from the village. I think we'd better give it a try."

It was non-stop work from that moment on. The letters didn't come through from Pencaster, so Pat could help as well. What a sawing and a banging came out of Ted's workshop all that day!

Before it was dark, the sledge was ready for a trial run. It went beautifully.

Granny Dryden saw it from
her windows, and thought
she was dreaming.
"I never saw the like of it since
I was a little girl!" she said.

They spent all the next morning practising with the sledge,
up to Peter Fogg's cottage, and down to the village. It took the
pony a while to get used to it, and they needed two for the uphill trip.
Ted changed the harness to allow for this, and fitted an extra set
of brakes to be sure.

At two o'clock, the ambulance was
waiting outside the Post Office.

Ten minutes later, the sledge arrived at the Foggs' cottage, with Mrs Pottage driving, and Pat working the brakes.

Doctor Gilbertson wrapped Jenny up in warm blankets,
and Peter helped her out to the sledge.
"All aboard!" shouted Pat, and they were off!

Slowly and smoothly they went gliding over the snow.
It was so deep that they went over the tops of the walls.
There was no need to follow the twisting road,
they just made a clear line down to the village.

Everyone who could get through the snow
was there to watch the sledge arriving.
A cheer went up as they came into sight,
and stopped next to the Pencaster ambulance.
Off went Peter and Jenny, with a wave
to all their friends.

The baby was born four days before Christmas.
Doctor Gilbertson went to see her in Pencaster Hospital,
taking cards and presents from everyone in Greendale.
"What a lovely little girl!" she said.
"Congratulations! What are you
going to call her?"
"Caroline," said Jenny.
"Our special snow-baby!"
"And she'll be home in
time for Christmas,"
said Doctor Gilbertson.

She was, but only just!
It was Christmas Day when baby Caroline came home.
The ambulance came as far as the village Post Office.
Pat and Mrs Pottage had the sledge ready, waiting for Jenny and
Caroline and Peter. There were piles of rugs to wrap them up
and keep them warm.

They all rode home together, with their presents
and a Christmas tree, piled in behind them.
The Greendale folk were there to greet them
and wave them on their way.

But there was something different about the sledge. Ted had done more work on it while Jenny had been in Pencaster.

As the ponies pulled the sledge up the hill, there was a musical ringing, sounding out across the snow! Ted had fitted a set of bells he had found, and polished up until they were like new.

What a home-coming for baby Caroline, on Christmas Day itself! "This," said Pat, as they drove the sledge back to Greendale Farm, "is one Christmas we will always remember."

The sledge was kept in the barn at Greendale Farm for many
a long year.

Every Christmas, when there was snow, Father Christmas arrived
in it, with a full load of presents for the children of the dale.

The children had rides across the snowy fields with the bells
ringing out.

Caroline Fogg sat in front, with Peter and Jenny, and had the first
sleigh-ride every year, just as she had that very first time she came
home to Greendale.